Jellybean Bo

Kittens Love

By Lisa McCue

Random House 🏠 New York

Library of Congress Catalog Card Number: 98-65751
ISBN: 0-679-89400-4 (trade) ; 0-679-99400-9 (lib. bdg.)

www.randomhouse.com/kids/

Printed in the United States of America   10 9 8 7 6 5 4 3 2 1

JELLYBEAN BOOKS is a trademark of Random House, Inc.

Kittens love...

to play with spools,

chase after pencils,

bat at yarn.

Kittens love

to roll
in catnip,

walk on
fences,

scramble up trees.

Kittens love

to lie in a heap
and squirm and wrestle.

Kittens love to nap…

in a patch of sunlight,

on the
Sunday paper,

in a basket
of fresh
laundry.

Kittens love
to hunt...

for mice
and bugs
and butterflies.

And when everyone else is fast asleep kittens love to explore the dark.

Kittens love to
sharpen their claws...

on the bark
of trees,

on the nap of
carpets,

on the brand-new drapes. No, no, kitty!

Kittens love
to lap
their milk

and keep
their fur
shiny clean.

Kittens love to sit
on the windowsill
for hours and hours
and watch birds.

But most of all,
kittens love
to curl up in
your warm
lap and purr...
and purr.